The Stone
& the Song

Ben Y. Faroe

First publication: Clickworks Press, 2015.
Release: CP-INT-P.CS-1.4

Sign up for production updates at byfaroe.com/updates.

ISBN: 978-0-692-41374-6

To Kristen, the queen of my heart
and the light of my eyes

The Stone and the Song

Dreams are but shades, we think, and smile,
And live in the firmness of day,
But Someone dreams a deeper truth
And life, as we wake, fades away.

As in a deep sleep I dreamt of a garden, a garden of flowers, a garden of stone. In that rich garden were mist-veiled blossoms, and in that lush garden were statues and fountains, and there in my dark heart a mystery was sown.

Alone in the garden there toiled a man. Before him, a woman of perfect white marble was standing and watching the tools in his hands as with chisel he chipped her and shaped her and smoothed her, perfecting her skirts and her smile and her hands. For many long years she had been his companion, and day after day he had worked to refine her, and night after night he would linger beside her, for there in the moonlight was magic and mystery. A hush fell on the edge of dusk. Under stars and under moon the marble lady slowly stretched. She yawned precisely, smiled brightly, then looked at him and took his hand. They walked a while, as flesh and stone, they wandered utterly alone. His other statues watched them nightly, some dark and some light, some merry, some sad, and though their presence cheered him slightly, though some could smile, or nod, or bow, not one gave comfort like his lady, and none had such an air of life.

Her mouth of stone could speak no word, no laugh escaped her pure white lips, but long ago he'd made a flute of purest white, and for himself a set of pipes, and there beneath the moon's dark eye on stony garden paths they'd meet, and hidden by the starry sky they'd play their haunting melody, and never was piping so sad, and never was piping so sweet.

———————·———————

Nearby in time, nearby in space, a small brown man sat choking in the dust of the street. His foot was lame and his face worn and scarred, but kind beneath its disfigurement. His eyes were striking, ice-blue, ice-clear. He sat alone, begging alms on the poor bright street. But sitting he watched, and watching he saw. Strange visions he saw, sights curious and deep, and in his clear eyes lay magic and mystery, and seeing he knew, and knowing he named, and he sang to those who passed by:

> "Sir, you are bound with a web of dark strings.
> Madam, a dove whispers words in your ear.
> Dear girl, you fly with an angel's bright wings.
> Ah, things are not as they appear!"

But seeing that he was scarred and lame, and seeing the haze in the bright dusty streets, they merely laughed or ignored him or whispered in pity as they passed.

"That poor muddled fakir, who knows what he dreams? So tired, so hungry, so hot, and so poor. At least his illusions afford him some comfort, but isn't it sad that he knows nothing more?"

All through the day he sat unheard and unwanted and entirely unable to stop seeing strange sights. Suddenly as he sat a tattered young man appeared in the dust at his side. The Fakir gave him a long steady look, and looking he saw, and seeing he sang:

> "Though poor you may be, on your head I can
>   see
> A helmet of steel, a proof against fear,
> Like the shield dark and strong I perceive in
>   your hand, for—"

"Things are not as they appear," said the youth

with a wink and a grin.

"Then you can see too?" cried the Fakir, amazed.

The youth just replied with a glint in his eye, "Seek the Company of the Broken."

And like dust on the wind he was gone.

The Fakir cocked his head and pondered this, but he could make nothing of it. Knowing the ways of such things, he tucked it away in his memory to await the day its meaning came.

Some time later, an old familiar urge tugged at him deep within. He closed his eyes to pay attention, and pausing he knew, and knowing, obeyed, with a quiet nod of his head. Slowly he rose to his tired old feet, and hobbled away with the wind at his side.

Up an obscure path on the side of a hill his laborious journey came to an end, and he knocked three times at a strong iron gate. He waited patiently, then, finding no reply, knocked again. After a few moments a man opened the gate and looked out quizzically. He was covered in dust and carrying a chisel, and behind him the Fakir saw a lush garden filled with many statues.

"You are the Sculptor. I bring you a message of life and death," said the Fakir, quite simply.

"Oh?" The man was confused, but not unkind.

"Your friends are not stones that lie shattered
    and dead.
The Dreamer invites you to realms of fierce joy.

A song among children is better than strength.
A life held too tightly is weaker than death."

"The Dreamer?"

"Yes. I expect you will learn of him later. For now,
hear his message:

'Your friends are not stones that lie shattered
   and dead.
The Dreamer invites you to realms of fierce joy.
A song among children is better than strength.
A life held too tightly is weaker than death.'

Will you remember this?"

"I...I don't know. Is it some sort of riddle?"

"I am only the messenger. I expect it will make
sense when it needs to. Now please repeat the
message. I must be sure you have learned it well."

"Very well, then," said the Sculptor uncertainly.
"My friends are not the rocks—"

"Not stones," corrected the Fakir.

"Not *stones* that are...broken, was it?"

"Your friends are not stones that lie shattered and
dead."

"My friends are not stones that lie shattered and
dead."

And so they continued, until the Fakir was
convinced that the Sculptor would not forget his
message.

"Well done," he said when they had finished. "Your willing heart has helped you more than you can understand today. Do not forget your message, and I hope we meet again one day." And with that he gave a curious, piercing smile and turned and began to hobble down the long road back into the heart of the city.

———————— · ————————

High above the city in a tower of the Princess's palace, a lone maiden sat watching the dust in the wind, as dusk crept quickly through the streets. Alone as she watched she played a dreaming song, a longing song, fragile on a silver flute. Suddenly a chill of worry took her, a strange premonition of loss and a sudden desperate sense of wrongness, and then, quick as it had come, it passed like a dream on the wind, leaving only a vague unease behind. She leapt up and ran to the door and flew down the stairs into the very heart of the palace, afraid for her dear mistress the Princess.

For many long years she had served her Princess and in adoration given all that she asked. Through years of quick and diligent obedience she had earned the Princess's love in return, and the Princess had kept her safe and secure in her tower high up in the air.

On many warm evenings the Princess had led her on wide, wandering paths in high-walled gardens, and many dim mornings the Princess had given her gifts of jewels and candies and clothes. And once in return for a fine silver flute and to show her devotion and love for her mistress and honor the years of their friendship the handmaid had given the Princess her voice, a soft small cocoon under fierce morning star. Then oft of an evening as they walked in the garden the Princess would sing a wordless duet. With both voices at once she would weave deep music and as she followed on dusk-laden flagstones the handmaid would listen, entranced with delight.

But now, driven by worry that had no name, she ran through the door, through thick heavy air, through rich marble halls and sought her dear lady and then at the throne room's door she skidded and stopped. She caught a deep breath and smoothed her hair and knocked three times on the thick loud door.

"Enter!" called a voice from within and the Voiceless Girl felt a wave of relief, and sighed, and smiled, and stepped inside, and a wind in the door caught her dark lovely hair.

Like a daughter of dawn, like a queen of the air, majestic and regal the Princess sat ruling with dazzling beauty and riches unknown. The city was hers and as sovereign she reigned, and would until in the passage of time none but the dust and the wind there remained. And seeing the fear in her handmaiden's eyes she laughed with delight and said, "Silly girl! Did you think I'd leave you?"

The Princess rose and walked to the window and peered over darkening streets.

"No, my men still continue the search. We have nothing but time, my girl, nothing but time."

And sitting again she began to sing a twin-voiced wordless song. Her song wove magic through the air, voice upon voice and song within song, and lulled the Voiceless Girl to sleep.

Asleep in the shade of the high palace wall in the land of the Dream walked the beggar in fear and groaned in his spirit as walking he saw a deep and familiar dark place. He tried to turn back, but his steps dragged him on to a time far away and a place long past.

And then the ravens began to gather and circle and swarm in the red broken air over red broken earth.

"You will never succeed!" they cackled and cawed. "We know you are lost! We say you are wrong! In weakness you will try to change, but we know what you *really* are."

He reached down and took hold of the broken red clay, and the vipers slid out of the cracks in the earth.

"You cannot succeed! Our mouths carry death. Your eyes carry lies. What you see will kill you one day."

He formed the clay into a mask, as silent as death, and then in the dream the ravens had settled, the snakes were beasts that crowded around.

"You are not one of us!" cried the soaring eagle.

The lion roared, "You are blind, you are dead!"

"We will spit you out!" growled a fearsome tiger. A great ram fiercely shook his horns.

He put on the mask, excited, afraid, and felt the clay become his flesh, and through its eyes he saw their masks, and seeing he knew, and knowing he named.

"You are the Company of the Reborn!" he cried aloud. "Yet you are but men like me!" His word echoed forth, resounding and strong, and its power began to crumble the masks.

"His magic will break us!" they snarled and they pounced, and cut him and beat him and tore off his mask. He screamed aloud as they hoisted him high and ran as a mob to the edge of the cliff where he clutched and resisted but their paws (or their fists?) pummeled him one last time and then he was thrown in a smooth, slow arc.

He fell and fell, in fear, in pain, and hit with an agonized crunch. Raw-faced, broken-legged, in the high cliff's shade, he looked up to see a man walking toward him with soft, measured tread, and as their eyes met, he saw and he named.

"You are the Dreamer, the king of true magic."

"I am the Dreamer, who sends out the winds. I bring you a warning of what I have dreamt: in the city an edict, a price on your head. Now flee to the wilderness, flee with the wind."

The beggar bowed low.

"I will do as you bid. Now my pain grows too great. Let me wake!"

And he did, with a twinge in his leg and cold scars on his face, and he wept with the pain of old wounds.

Yet the Dreamer's warm voice re-echoed in waking, "A price on your head, now flee!"

———— · ————

As midnight neared, the Sculptor walked with his White Lady as in a dream. He spoke to her his fondest heart, and through the hours she listened close with glinting eyes and winning smile. Then for a time they played again, the music as ever sad and sweet, and finally the hour came, and she stepped up on her pedestal, and smiled at him, and was still.

Scarcely had he turned away from a last longing gaze when a clang rang—sudden, rough! A clanging at the gate! A screech of tearing hinges!

Held back by fear, he crouched behind the White

Lady's pedestal and peered around the edge. More noises, thick boots stomping rustle-crush as plants and branches cracked. Then the clank-clank of dented metal and glass smash-shatter-scattering— his sculptures! In angry disbelief the Sculptor leapt from his hiding place and ran, shouting, around a bend in the garden path. The sight dropped him still like a boot to the gut.

Six burly goons ransacked his garden, trampling plants and overturning statues left and right. The thick iron bars of his gate hung twisted and useless at a wild angle. Before his eyes one of the goons lifted a kindly old mahogany man, still in his rocking chair, and smashed him to the ground in a shower of splinters. The Sculptor screamed reflexively, "No!" and reached out, but two huge men grabbed him in rock-like arms and held him fast. The others continued to fan out, leaving shredded leaves and shattered statues in their wake, and then with sudden slow clarity, he saw one turn and point at his ever-beloved White Lady, and time continued its sickening crawl.

In panic and desperation he screamed and struggled, but so hard was he held that he nearly wrenched his arms from their sockets—and would have, long before he broke the behemoth grip. He cried out pleas and promises in a tumble of hurried words, but the huge man before him only turned, and smiled, and then with a club hard as reality he struck the elegant White Lady a shattering blow. In a flash he reached into the wreckage and snatched up a smooth white heart and lifted it high and gave a hard laugh, and in moments they were gone again, and the night fell dark and still.

The Sculptor collapsed in wrenching sobs, then in anguish he stumbled and scrabbled half-blind through all the shattered remains. He found her face some paces from the pedestal. Her last gentle smile was broken in two. Her flute by her feet remained intact.

He gave it a long look, then took it up and swore on it an oath to take back the heart that had animated his White Lady and create her once again though it take the rest of his life, then he looked out over the ruin of his garden and wept many bitter tears.

When his tears were spent he rose sharply and turned deep into the garden, to the wild and trackless places even he rarely went, and found there a mammoth block of obsidian, far greater than he, and climbing upon it and dashing around it he started to carve it in great slashing blows. Huge sheets and blocks of the dark glassy stone fell away and shattered in razor fragments as the Sculptor poured all of his darkness, rage, hatred, and fear into the cold stone, and soon there emerged the form of a jagged, raw, hulking gargoyle. Blade-edged wings towered high over crooked horns. Its wicked dagger claws were swords of heartless dark. And deep in the deep dark deep in the center of the cruel dark beast born of pain the horror of its dark obsidian heart flashed sharp with the deep dark night.

On through the night the Sculptor raged, barely watching his creation take shape. The garden resounded with loud crushing and smashing as he worked in blind fury and despair, and always, like a crystal rain, the continual tinkling of shards falling to the ground and shattering again. At times he wept anew and howled heedless in raw grief, at times he muttered madly, or shouted dark curses on those who had torn and shattered his beautiful life. With fiendish energy he worked, with endurance born of raw emotion. Then, at last, at the first colorless yawn of morning light, his strength left him, and in a dead faint he fell from the monster he had carved and lay in the shards below.

At the sun's first gleam the gargoyle's deep heart flared. It shook itself roughly with a raucous clatter, then with crooked agility it scuttled up the garden wall and perched for a moment, overlooking the city with baleful eye. Then its wings snapped open with an ear-shattering crack and it leapt high into the air above the city.

As dawn broke over the city the Fakir hobbled toward the wide city gates. He watched two guards swing them slowly open. He began to approach, when one of the guards nailed to one huge wooden door a sign with a surprisingly accurate drawing of the Fakir's scarred face and the legend:

WANTED
for the Crimes of
Sorcery
and
High Treason
REWARD

With a gasp he drew back into an alleyway. Someone tapped him on the shoulder. He started and whirled around to see the young man from the day before.

"You!"

"Follow me."

The young man began a brisk walk to a nearby section of the wall and began to sing in a rich voice.

"O Dreamer, O Singer,
O Dancer of Wind,
Reveal now the gateway
To let our friend in."

They looked for a moment, then the young man

cried "There!" and pointed to where the wind whistled through a narrow cleft in the rocks. "There is the way to freedom!"

"Friend, I thank you," said the beggar. "But what is your name?"

"I, too, dream the Dream, and we sing the same Song, and that is all that matters. Now go quickly. Drink deep of the stream you find, for it will sustain you in the desert."

The Fakir nodded and turned to squeeze through the narrow gate, and was surprised to find how easily he passed through. Beyond it was a small vale of tender green grass fed by a cool crystal stream. He hobbled to the little stream and drank a small sip. He gasped at its fresh and delectable flavor, and splashed its cool fragrance over his head, hands, and feet. So rich and refreshing, invigorating and clean was the water that even the one brief sip seemed it must be enough to sustain him for hours, forever, for life. He crossed the cool stream to climb the small rise beyond. When he reached the peak he looked out and his heart melted at the sight before his eyes. As far as his eyes could see was heat and death, and no path was in sight in that whole trackless waste. He took a long look back at the strong city walls, but knowing nothing remained there but bondage and death he sighed a deep sigh and set out.

———— · ————

The Sculptor woke slowly in the high sun's glare. He lay for a moment with his eyes closed, haunted by a vague nightmare. An odd burning pain covered his body. He opened his eyes and saw all around him a chaos of razor obsidian shards, and it all came back to him in an instant. He sat up slowly, with dried blood tugging his clothes to the ground and gasped as a hundred lacerations burned awake across his body. The air lay heavy on his torn and broken garden. The gargoyle was nowhere to be seen. Scarcely had he taken it in when there was a rough clanging at the iron gate.

Afraid the goons were back, he struggled to his feet and began limping toward the garden's entrance, his fuzzy mind desperately seeking a plan. However, at the twisted gate he found no tough giants of men, but a smartly-dressed captain and a division of soldiers. The captain produced a small scroll and announced.

"You are wanted for the slaughter of the Princess's personal guard and the abduction of the Princess. You will come with us to await trial and execution."

"But I haven't...I don't know what you mean!" cried the Sculptor.

"You deny the charges?"

"Yes!"

"Then I have no choice but to use force." The captain smiled a cruel smile and raised a slow hand in signal to his men. They advanced menacingly, spears at the ready.

With a sudden crack and clatter, a gigantic shadow fell from the sky and scattered the men like toys. With a swift blow from one razor-edged wing, in a sudden spray of blood, the gargoyle swept away several soldiers, and before the rest could react it snatched up the Sculptor and leapt high in the air and flapped away in a cacophony like shattering stone, off toward the vast dry waste.

———·———

The Voiceless Girl awoke in a stream of terrifying sunlight as a mighty wind rushed through the room, rattling the door and howling through every crack and chink in her walls. In fear she arose, she flew to the door and as she opened it a tiny crack, the wind swept it wide open and she tumbled through. The castle felt suddenly empty, swept bare by the violent passion of the wind. She began to explore tentatively, working her way from room to room, strangely reluctant to reach the throne room.

Chamber by chamber she searched the stronghold, and in the eerie silence she found nothing but the hidden whispers of the wind. Finally, with a deep breath and a thrill of fear, she crept into the depths of the castle and gave a sudden shriek at what she saw. The throne room doors were wide open, hanging drunk off twisted hinges, and there in the wide hallway lay the remains of six hulking bodyguards, violently torn and strewn about like broken toys. Seeing them laid out in such vile manner, sensing the new reek of corruption about them, she wavered, stumbled, but a fresh breeze cleared her mind and with grim resolve she passed through the gore-wet door of the castle's dark throne room.

An appalling disarray met her gaze. Nothing was where it had been, and the trappings and tapestries were shredded away, the walls strangely bare, the statues shattered. The rich heavy curtains and strong majestic shutters were slashed apart, and now the fierce wind sang freely through the room and the halls. Impossibly, the marble floor was covered with gigantic taloned footprints, dug deep as if the stone were soft mud, tracing the frenzied rampage that had destroyed the room and finally leading out a grand window whose thick stone sill was entirely torn away.

But the greatest shock lay in the center of the room. The Princess, her Lady, the queen of her heart, was gone, leaving nothing but a gash of claws and a brooding wind hovering over the great throne.

Chilled by the sudden emptiness, she ran about the room closing the remains of the great shutters to soften the wind as well as she could, then fell to the floor in a daze. The palace was irrevocably changed, and the turmoil of her heart made it feel suddenly foreign, no longer her home.

She leapt to her feet and fled to the dusty streets outside and ran and stumbled until she found herself passing through the wide city gate into the deep wilderness beyond. And there in the heat of the sun-pounded sands she heard on the heavy air a glimmer of an echo of a twin-voiced song, and that wordless song consumed the confusion of her mind and gave her a desperate dark hope, and with angry resolve she set out to find her Princess and rescue her from whatever beast or man had captured her away.

———— · ————

For long hours the dark stone monster swept over the hot wild sands with the helpless Sculptor clutched tight in its dark claws, until from the constant crushing clatter of its wings and the furnace blast of the burning desert air and the relentless grip of its hard dark talons he'd lost all sense of place or direction.

After unknown time had passed, a soft wind revived his ears with the echo of a distant song. Faint as it was, he felt his spirit reviving and his mind beginning to clear under its influence. At the same moment, the beast that held him gave a grunt and a gravelly roar of rage and swiftly wheeled around to wing its way toward the source of the song.

———————•———————

The Fakir limped through the desert on blistered feet. He choked on the dust that the empty wind threw in his face and thought longingly of the stream he had drunk from outside the city walls. Here in the wilderness there was no water in sight, no relief from the heat, no path in the shifting sands. He was entirely alone, and soon in his lonely desperation he heard in every whistling gust of wind sweet words spoken to him alone, whispers of comfort amid the gusts of furnace-blast passion.

Soon he realized that what he heard was no longer the wind, but a haunting song of intertwined voices. Though they spoke no words, he seemed to hear in the enchanting duet promises of cool fresh water, of lush grass and pleasant company. Almost unaware, he turned to shuffle slowly in the direction of the song. The hard wind began to buffet him and push him off the path he'd chosen, but now the wild wind's whistles held no false words for him, and made fierce by the desires the song had burned into his heart, he turned his face against the wind and struggled on to find its source.

The haunting call of the wind in the desert was the Voiceless Girl's only companion as she chased the hollow echo of the Princess's song. She felt faint and famished and thirsty above all, but always the mingled wordless music drew her on, just out of reach, just over the next hill, promising joy and restoration, rest and refreshment and cool fresh water if she could only move her feet faster, push harder, finally catch up to the Princess she loved.

She worked all the harder, strove and pushed, hour after hour until sweat had permeated her clothes and her feet were burning and her mouth was utterly dry, and slowly the song grew clearer until she heard the Princess singing with both of their voices together, so close she knew they must be mere moments apart.

A fresh gust of burning wind caressed her wandering hair, and on it she heard a new song, the voices of children singing of water, of life. The words of their song tempted her gaze, and looking she saw a hazy pool forming on the sands where they stood. As she watched, it seemed to grow and glisten, and her heart cried out for the relief it offered. But the song of the Princess was so close, so close, and as she hesitated it took on a plaintive tone in her ears and a desperate urgency drew her attention back and her feet trudged on in their long habit as she turned back to chase her elusive mistress.

And then, almost dead in the toil of her pursuit, she crested a final dune and there in the valley was the Princess. Almost too faint to cry out for joy, almost too weak to bear her relief, the Voiceless Girl tumbled down the hill of dust and fell at her knees before the Princess, and the twin-voiced song rang strong in her ears and the power of it suddenly overwhelmed her anew as the Princess looked down on her.

The girl looked up, and a chill ran through her as she realized that there were no captors, no beast, no one in sight but the dark and powerful lady before her. The song fell silent as a look of shock grew on the Princess's face. For a long moment silence hung heavy as the hot desert air, and the song of the singing children wafted gently between them.

"You?" cried the Princess, and the girl smiled brightly and struggled to stand, but as she unsteadily reached her feet, a blinding slap across her face dropped her back to her knees.

"Fool!" shouted the Princess. "Wretched slave!"

And though the Voiceless Girl was too weak to look up, too soaked in sudden pain, she could hear the disgust curling across her Lady's lips.

"Could you not see that I had no more use for you?" she screamed, and something sharp like talons sliced the girl's flesh as with another brutal slap she laid her in the sand.

As the girl lay sobbing, bleeding, the light and the life slowly fading from her eyes, the Princess—no, the Witch, the Sorceress—raged and laughed and mocked the Voiceless Girl with her own stolen voice until finally, mercifully, all had faded to darkness and silence.

———— • ————

The gargoyle sped through the darkening sky in chase of the song that seemed to enrage it. As they grew closer, the Sculptor began to revive, and soon he could hear the words of the song and the joyful harmony of many children's voices. As the children came into view beside a small, fresh oasis, a strong wind arose and buffeted the monster back, but its dark obsidian heart flashed with malevolent energy and the stony beast battled the wind with a gravelly roar and the shattering clatter of its huge stony wings.

The wind kept resisting, laced with the children's clear song, but the gargoyle grew only angrier and stronger, fueled with hate for the children who stood so close but just out of reach. It gained little ground but fought on all the harder, when suddenly a shift in the wind's current swept it forward and in a flash it reached the singing children and before it had even skittered to a halt in the burning sand its razor-sharp wing lashed out in a sweeping slash of violent rage. The Sculptor gasped, still clenched in the stony sharp talons and half-buried in the gritty hot sand, but the children never flinched.

With a jarring shock, the wing stopped short as it hit the first child's tender neck, and with an ear-splitting crack a large piece of it splintered and rained down onto the sand. The child, unharmed, sang on as he stepped forward to lay a soft hand on the great stone monster. The gargoyle shrieked in rage and lashed out again, but the child he hit was likewise unhurt and another large piece of the gargoyle's wing shattered and fell in a sprinkle of crystalline shards, and now all the children began to step forward one by one, side by side, and quietly lay their hands on their ineffectively brutal attacker.

In a growing frenzy of rage the monster struck out against them, but nothing seemed able to break their delicate skin. A swift blow that should have beheaded a tiny girl outright sent a huge stone wingtip spinning through the air to land many yards away. Attempts to gore their small bodies simply pulverized the beast's sharp horns. The harder it hit, the more damage it did to itself, while the children stood firm against the brutal assault.

And on and on they sang. Individual children fell into silence now and again, but always the song went on, and the silences were as deeply a part of the song's rich harmonies as the singing. They sang strange words, bold words, words of too much strength for children so small and weak.

Soon the dark monster had nothing left to strike with, nothing except the deadly talons that still held the Sculptor fast. Stripped of its horns and wings, standing amidst its own shattered remains, the beast glared balefully with obsidian eyes and the dark heart flashed malevolently at the statue's core as it roared and growled with dangerous passion.

And now the children's song shifted and they began to sing with a mystical, ferocious gentleness, a power all the more forbidding for the restraint in which it was continuously held. Slowly, deliberately, inexorably, some began to reach down and wrap their tiny fingers around the massive razor claws of the towering beast, and the stone crumbled to powder in their gentle grasp, and they broke off the wretched talons one by one until the Sculptor was free.

Meanwhile, another group of children began to tear out chunks of the monster's stone body until they had burrowed down to its huge dark heart. With careful firmness, they drew it out into the light and before the Sculptor's marveling gaze they smoothed the dark, sharp stone into a strong shield with razor edges, and this they handed to the astonished Sculptor.

"Who are you?" he cried out, finding his haggard voice at last. "And how do you have such power?"

> "Our names are nothing,
> Our power is weak.
> To know the Dreamer
> Is to know the Dream.
> His Song holds power.
> His words hold truth.
> To dream the Dream
> Is to hear the Song.
> To sing the Song
> Is to build the Dream."

"What is this dream, and how do you stand so strong?"

"Our strength lies in our helmets. You need one too."

"Where are these helmets? How can I make one?"

The children shook their heads sagely.

"Any helmet you make will break. Only the Dreamer can give you a true helmet. You must ask him!"

"How I ask him when I can't even see him?"

They smiled.

"We will teach you." And they sang for him, a song of the Dream, a song of such depth and longing and beauty that his very heart thirsted for it, and in yearning he cried out, "What is this great Dream? I must see, I must sing!"

And the children sang out in time with his plea, "O Dreamer, O Dancer, O Singer of Life, let him see! Let him see!"

They pointed with joy at the desert's bare dunes.

"There, can you see it?" And gleeful grins broke out on their faces.

"Is it not lovely?" A dance began to simmer in the tingling crowd.

"Can you not see it?" The air stood on tiptoe, the song held its breath, and in the lush silence the Sculptor looked out, and slowly, so slowly, he saw.

There on the dunes was the dream of a forest. A fresh, tumbling river ran through the dry dust. The sands shimmered green with the breath of new life.

"I see it! I see it!"

"You see it! Now sing!"

And he sang loud and strong, and the dance boiled over. For an hour, for a year, for a moment they danced as the thrill of the song rang in them and through them. The wind rushed round them and lifted their song. Like flames they danced and leapt and shone, with joy transcendent, with joy unknown, with rollicking, tumbling, shimmering laughter their song overflowed for the Dreamer alone, 'til slowly the stars joined the dance and the Song.

In due time they finished the dance. An older

child stepped forward and spoke. "Now quickly, we must move on."

The younger children bowed slightly and began walking toward the low sunset, their song unbroken. A small contingent, acting on no instructions the Sculptor could hear, ran ahead and were soon out of sight. The older child, seemingly the troop's leader, pulled the Sculptor aside as they walked and spoke in a hushed voice.

"You would do well to come with us. There is a sign in the Song. Soon I fear you must face a great pain, and the necessary preparations must be made."

"But what of this great celebration we have shared?"

"There is a time for dancing and a time to do battle, my friend, and one does not diminish the need for the other. Or did you not see that we are soldiers as well as singers?" He pointed at the crowd of small children, and the Sculptor looked on them again. They appeared normal at first, but as soon as he remembered to look for the Dream, he saw that they all wore ethereal helmets and in their tiny hands he saw glittering sharp swords and shields of varying sizes.

"But they are only children!" exclaimed the Sculptor.

"True, but the Dreamer is ageless and ancient. He dreams the truth, and we need only watch the Dream and stand firm."

"I don't understand."

"You will begin to understand when you begin to fight. It is hard to see the Dream until you find your place in it, and even then it can be elusive. That is why the Dreamer has given us the Song. The Song need never stop. The Song is a great comfort in darkness and battle. I advise you to learn it well."

"And when I have learned it—" The Sculptor's gaze drifted, and he took hold of the white marble flute that he kept by his heart. His face hardened. "Then will I be able to win back my Lady's heart?"

The youth looked at him long and hard, and the Sculptor heard him humming faintly. A curious look came into his eyes, and he slowly shook his head.

"You will indeed win the heart of the lady you seek, but she is not your white lady, and the fight will not be what you think."

After that they spoke of many things as they journeyed back to the children's camp, and the youth taught him many mysteries of the Dream and the Song, but any time the Sculptor spoke of his White Lady, the youth would smile and shake his head, happy and sad, and say no more on the subject.

———— · ————

The sun hung low in the sky as the Fakir continued to struggle through the desert, drawn on by the intoxicating duet that seemed to ring out only for him. Thirst and hunger and raw exhaustion hounded him, but the song, though wordless, seemed to promise him food and fresh water and deep, lasting rest.

Unable to stop, he trudged on into the night, enchanted by the magical melody streaming around him. It seemed to envelop him, to carry him on—or at least keep his feet moving—and all his mind was consumed by the joy he would find when he finally reached the singer.

Once, briefly, the song had stopped, and the beggar had almost succumbed to his need for sleep, but just as he'd found what comfort he could in the rough sand, just as he seemed finally on the edge of rest, the song began again, and he realized what he had been about to do, and quickly rose to his feet and limped twice as fast to make up for his folly, and the day slowly sank into darkness.

———————·———————

Long hours later the Sculptor and the band of children crested a dune and there, in a vale, in a dark pool of blood lay a deadly pale maiden draped in lovely dark hair. Around her sat the forerunner children, who sat in the dust in the dusk as they sang. They sang strong and sad, strong and soft, strong in life, but the young woman lay between them weak and white as the dead. Two of the children ran to greet the Sculptor.

"You have come at last! The Dreamer sang to us of your arrival, but even so some of us were beginning to despair. Now come quickly. She is resting, but her time is short."

"She?" The Sculptor looked at the youth beside him, and saw the same inscrutable look in his eyes.

The young man spoke with quiet intensity.

"It seems your battle is upon you even sooner than expected, Sculptor."

The Sculptor approached the dying woman, hesitant, almost reverent, and gasped to see deep gashes like claw marks across one pale cheek. Beside her sat a young girl, tending her with a quiet song.

"You can save her," said the girl. "But it will not be easy. The choice is yours. We won't think less of you if you choose not to." A sober quietness fell as the heavy breeze danced over the fearful death in their midst.

"What must I do?"

The girl matched his gaze steadily, her eyes deadly serious.

"Her heart has been destroyed. If she is to be saved, you must give her your own heart, and take hers in its place. It will cause you great pain, perhaps even death, but it is the only way. We will sing over you to reduce the pain and bring what healing we can, but even so you will never be the same."

The Sculptor stood a moment in silence as the enormity of the question before him slowly sank in, and his heart desperately sought another way.

"Can you not sing your healing over her?" he asked.

"Not for very much longer. A broken heart in a weak body cannot survive for long. A broken heart in a strong body, a strong heart in a weak body, these may perhaps be restored to fullness of life."

"But why must I do it? Surely there must be another better suited than I!" But even as the words left his mouth, he knew them to be false and cowardly, and was ashamed.

"No one else has your gifts, or your place in the Dream. You are a builder of life, are you not? When will you stop wasting your gifts on cold stone?"

The Sculptor sank into perplexed silence as she continued.

"To give one's life to another, that is the wildest and strongest dream by far, and few and privileged are those who may sing it. Indeed, that is the dark and lovely song the Dreamer sings, and some say it is the source of all his vast joy. Now consider carefully what you will do, but do not wait too long or the choice will no longer be yours to make."

"How can I know?" cried the Sculptor. "Do not put this burden on me!"

The youth at his side smiled small and tired.

"Look to the Dream, friend. Always look to the Dream."

The Sculptor looked, but the night was dark, and hard as he looked, and soft as he looked, there was no dream, no life, no sign.

"I see nothing!" he whispered in a sudden panic, as before him the girl spilled her life on the sand.

He looked again, and cold reality tore at him, no dream, only faces that stared at him.

"What can I do?" he cried.

"The Dream—"

"It's not there!"

"It is always—"

"No!" And now darkness overwhelmed him and he grabbed the young man. "I cannot save her! I can see nothing!"

"Friend—"

"My friends are the stones that lie shattered and dead!" Then he stopped, amazed. "No. My friends are not stones that lie shattered and dead. The Dreamer invites me to realms of fierce joy. A song among children is better than strength. A life held too tightly is weaker than death."

He paused on the vertiginous edge of soul-defining decision, and found himself calm.

"I have made my choice," he said. And he sang, faltered, hesitant, shy. But he knew as he sang, as a flute knows the wind, as a wave knows the sea, for as soon as his voice sang the Song sang in him, like the ring of the tang of a fine strong sword. And he looked upon the dying maiden and a sudden tenderness filled his heart, and the Song surged through him anew. "Now sing for me, friends, for the path before me is dark indeed."

Then the whole camp sang a powerful song, a mystery song of healing in pain, a paradox song of dying in life and living in death, and the Sculptor sang with them and the Song was true. His heart raced within him as he took up his great shield and with its razor tip he stabbed the beautiful girl in the chest. She twitched, and a tear rolled down her smooth cheek. With tears in his eyes, he stabbed her again, and her body convulsed, but her eyes remained shut as his tears fell like rain. A third time he cut deep into her flesh, and three bright lines of blood surrounded her heart, and she sighed a deep sigh as if troubled in sleep, and he lowered his shield and wept in deep and wrenching anguish.

And then, drenched in tears and in blood and in deathly cold sweat, the Sculptor lifted his shield once again, and the dark stone flashed as he faced its sharp end. With a great shout, he plunged it deep into his chest and gasped in magnificent pain. Again he stabbed, and he fell to his knees and the world was dimmed in a flash of red. But the Song raged around him and his strength was renewed, and with a desperate cry he cut once more, deep into himself, and he reeled and would have fallen if the hands of many children had not reached out to hold him steady.

With the last of his strength he tore out his heart and gave it to her, and took her weak heart inside himself, and then he fell to the earth as if dead, and for a long moment all his world was the tide of the Song and the dance of the wind and the touch of a hundred tiny hands, until all fell into darkness and silence.

———— · ————

In the heart of the desert, in the depth of the night, the hunt of the Fakir finally ended. At the peak of a great dune stood the one who had reeled him in with the wordless power of her song. And now he could see that her promises were nothing, but it was too late, and he fell to his knees in despair. In a flash she leapt, so high and so still that she seemed to fly, to ride the heavy desert air, and she landed beside him and hissed a dark tune, and he saw that he was bound in chains. She laughed a harsh and reckless laugh, and the broken Fakir dropped his gaze.

"Look at me!" she commanded, and his helpless head snapped up. "Look on me, the mistress of life! By your gaze you will complete my power, and I shall live to reign forevermore!"

"None will reign forever but the Dreamer, and he

is the one true master of life!" The Fakir spat in the sand and turned away.

"Look at me!" screamed the Sorceress again, and as his head jerked back a burst of heat flashed in his chains and seared his flesh. "I know your dreamer. He chases invisible dreams, fantasies of hope. They will lead him to the same ruin they have brought on you. But I have found the true secret of life. No dream, no vague hope and children's lullaby, but this!"

She reached into her cloak and pulled out a white marble heart.

"This is reality. This is life. Touch it. See it. It is firm, it is strong. *This* is truth, not that dancer's mad dream. Others may throw their fate to the wind, but I hold mine in my own two hands."

"You would entrust your life to a dead stone? Your foolishness is great indeed!"

"Silence! Your wisdom is foolishness. Can a stone die? Will solid stone tear and rot like dying flesh? You are blind, and you will perish in your lack of vision. And yet you are not wholly blind, for I know of your gift. What you see is truth, is it not?"

The Fakir gave her a dark look.

"Most say I see only fantasies."

"Fantasies indeed, but even a beggar's dreams may have their use." She held out the heart of stone. "This heart is from a most marvelous statue. It has been given the touch of life. Look upon it, see it alive, that it may live indeed."

"What you ask is impossible!" The Fakir stared at her hand in shock. "There is no life there. I cannot see what is not there!"

"Indeed!" cried the Sorceress, and a manic gleam entered her eye. "You cannot see falsehood, so see the life in this heart and it will truly live!"

"There is no life!" insisted the Fakir. "Can life come from death?"

"Can death come from life?" screamed the Sorceress. "Yes! Why not life from death? Life and death are one, and I hold its key here in my hand. A living stone will never die."

"Nothing truly lives that cannot die," said the Fakir, and he fixed her with a fearsome glare.

"And yet your dreamer lives," her voice sank to an intense, victorious whisper. "And even so, by your word he shall die."

At the vicious force of her final word, the Fakir fell in a faint, but her hand seized his face in a death grip, and beneath her smooth fingertips broke deep slashes in his flesh, and in the shock of pain his eyes opened again, and she held the cold stone before his helpless gaze, and laughed in the sheer dark thrill.

His head shook and his mouth gave muffled cries through her hard hand, but his wide fearful eyes were held by the smooth hard stone before him, and soon a wicked smile twisted the Sorceress's lips.

In the heavy silence a new song began to drift

over them, a man's rich voice singing life and truth. The Sorceress hesitated, paled, but then her confidence returned.

"No!" she laughed, and her eyes were hard. "They are too late. It is finished!"

And a man and a beautiful woman rounded the hilltop, and the Song washed around them.

"You are too late!" screamed the Sorceress. "Your power is nothing. You have already lost."

The Sculptor ignored her and spoke to the Fakir. "You know she is wrong. She is destroying what little life she has. Look again to the Dreamer, friend. The Dream is life, the Song is truth. Look on her no longer, for she has no power over you."

Then the Voiceless Girl touched his eyes, and pointed to his chains, and the Fakir came to his senses and began to see again, and he saw that the heavy chains were draped over his wrists and lay upon his ankles, but no shackles held him, and he raised his hands and labored to his feet, and the thick strong chains fell to the earth. The Sorceress opened her cruel mouth and raised a cruel hand, but the Sculptor turned to her and she paused. He held her eye as he hummed a soft tune for several long moments. And waiting he saw, and seeing he smiled, and he spoke words quiet and bold.

"I sing the Song, I watch the Dream. Today is your downfall. This man is free and you will not have him." His smile turned dark. "And you cannot keep my Lady."

His words held such power that for a moment the Sorceress stood stunned and silent. The Sculptor's voice rang out in song and he touched the pile of chains, then lifted it from the ground as a thick and mighty shield, and this he gave to the Fakir. Then the Sorceress recovered, and gave a derisive laugh.

"Take him," she spat. "I have no further use for him. Indeed, I need nothing more. The hour of my victory is at hand!"

She began to chant dark and powerful words, and in the heavy hiss of her cruel incantation they saw her as she truly was: old, old as the ancient rocks and hills, with hollow eyes sunk deep and turned inward, and sharp bony hands like razor-point claws, and feet like a great vulture's talons.

"It was you!" cried the Sculptor. "You killed your own guard!"

"And drove me away from the city," said the Fakir.

"And arranged for my arrest and execution." The Sculptor stared at her. "But why?"

"I have found all I need," she snarled, raising the stone heart high. "As for the rest, why not?"

"My lady's heart!" snarled the Sculptor and made to leap at her.

She beckoned him once with her sharp, taloned hands, and laughed, and slashed at the air, and he fell back in fear. At that she gave a dark cackle and took up her chant once more.

The Sculptor and the Fakir sang to resist her, but their song only seemed to add power to her transformation, and soon she stood before them hideous, a monstrous echo of an evil person, and then a second voice began to sing, and the Sculptor's new heart leapt within him and words burst out of his mouth.

"That is not your voice!"

"You are wrong," laughed the Sorceress, and she pointed with scorn at the Voiceless Girl. "She gave it to me long ago, and I have swallowed it up. It is deep within me, and you shall never have it again."

The Girl glared at her with fire in her eyes, and out of the Sculptor's mouth burst "No!" and the Sorceress paused and snarled, "Stay back, girl. You have no place here."

"Be silent," the Sculptor's voice spoke with clear authority as the Girl stared her down. "I have been your slave for far too long. Now I am free. You will not deceive me, and you will release my voice."

"You are pitiful and dark," snapped the Sorceress. "Do not speak to me with that false voice." And with the Girl's own voice she began to laugh, cruel and mocking.

"Be silent," repeated the Sculptor's voice. "I am dark but lovely. You do not know me, and you must release my voice."

"You have no voice!" laughed the Sorceress. "You

gave it away. Years ago, too many years in forgotten days. You chose to give it away. You despised it and gave it to me. You have no claim to it and you do not deserve it." And again she mocked in the Girl's own voice. "Worthless and ugly, stupid and dull, you are the source of the pain and the fear. Dreadful, inadequate, useless, and weak. I name you Deceived. I name you Defeat. I name you the Destitute, drained of all peace. Dreamless you wander and lifeless you fall."

With every insult the Girl cringed and wept, and slowly she sank to her knees in the sand, and the Sculptor beside her cried, "Stop, please stop," in a piteous voice accustomed to pain. Then—

"Stop!" And he planted his shield hard in the sand. "The Dreamer would speak to his daughter."

And the Song rang through him in power and he sang.

"Bountiful beauty, I name you Beloved, I name you Victorious, I name you Untroubled. Your voice is for singing, for power and truth. Your voice is for freedom and wisdom and youth. In joy overflowing I look on your face for angels will envy the joy you will taste. In wonder you dream and unfailing you live. You will outlast the sun, you will stride among stars, and in glory I'll crown you and clothe you in light. Accepted and radiant, my pride and my pleasure, my sister, my love, and my dazzling treasure. To gates of death and beyond I'll pursue you. When you fall in your weakness I'll fight to renew you. Your fears will pass, your faults will wane, and today, now, in the presence of your enemy, I release your voice."

"Lies!" cried the Sorceress, weak and aghast. With fierce resolve and bitter tenacity she shouted again, "Foolish lies! My victory is here!" And her evil chant resumed, and with the Girl's voice she sang the first deep notes of the healing song.

But "Not so!" cried the Fakir, and he sang strong and clear.

> "A small cocoon, a tiny death,
> A fluttering life, a shining breath,
> And stolen life shall flee from fear
> For things are not as they appear."

But she ignored him and sang on, and they recognized the healing song, but shuddered, for she sang no words and it fell hollow and twisted on their ears. But still her evil chant carried on. The Sculptor's heart burned to hear the voice so fouled, and the Voiceless Girl paled as if in pain, but the Fakir laid his hands on them and spoke, quiet, now, and strong.

"Stand firm, friends, for I see her undoing."

Into the sand they planted their shields, shield of chain and shield of stone, and all three leaned on them and stood together, and watched in terrible wonder.

For soon the Sorceress began to falter and her song broke apart and her body convulsed. Then she fell to her knees and her head jerked back and out of her throat poured a storm of butterflies, brilliant, vibrant, swirling, and wild. They flew on the wind. They sought the Girl. They sought the one who held her heart. And drawn they landed, on him and on her, and covered their bodies like feathers on skin, and settled, and rested, and then melted into their hands and their faces, their arms and their feet, and in rapture the Girl sang aloud.

"Love and laughter sing in me and I am free again, again! The Dream is rich in me, in me, and I can sing again, again."

And then with a rippling laugh, a shimmering laugh, she pulled out her small silver flute.

"Farewell, false voice!" And she threw it away into the sands, and before their eyes it melted into a mirror puddle of silver, and her song rang out all the merrier.

But as she sang the Sorceress laughed again, a cackling, coughing laugh, and slowly rose to her feet.

"You have not won yet!" she shrieked. "You have stolen my ability to sing healing as I chant, yes. I can no longer ward off the pain of my plan." She paused, and in the hanging silence her sneer—if it were possible—grew even more cruel. "But I am no stranger to pain."

And she cried out her dark incantation and the

deathly talons flashed into sight again, and with a wild and dismal cry she plunged her claws deep into her own breast and tore out a crimson heart of flesh, and crushed it, and it dropped to the sand as she fell to her knees. With a last wheezing laugh she filled the gaping wound in her chest with the white heart of stone, and her dark blood drenched its smooth innocence.

"I have won!" she screamed, and she shook a bloody fist at the heavy heavens. "I, *I* have done it and no other! Now my victory shall be complete and final." And she poured forth the healing song's melody with all the power of her fell voice, and a triumphant smile grew on her curled crimson lips.

The three behind the shields watched in mounting horror.

"She doesn't know the words!" gasped the Sculptor. And now all three could see her skin slowly turn gray as death crept through her body. Her eyes began to widen in panic, and her song rose in horrified urgency, but to no avail. Her flesh began to shrivel, and the Girl turned away in tears. And now the voice of the dying Sorceress grew shrill in a final screech of fear and weakness, and she fell to the sand, her dead stone heart still visible in her torn dead chest.

The Girl sobbed uncontrollably as the Sculptor let out a long, shuddering sigh and the Fakir merely shook his head numbly, dazed by the dark and terrible visions that had accompanied her death. For a time the three simply wept together, then broke out in a wailing dirge, and they sang and sang of pain and loss, and the Song's cathartic power burned within them, until all three fell exhausted to sleep amid the lonely sands.

They awoke in glad sunshine to the sound of children's voices. Around them thronged the singing children, and the Girl smiled brightly.

"Then we have won!" she laughed. "We are free indeed!"

The Fakir looked about him at the crowd of children, examining them carefully with his piercing blue eyes.

"You are the Company of the Broken!" he cried, suddenly understanding. "Yet you are mere men like me!"

"And in our eyes you are but a child, with many years yet to spend with us," replied the children, and the Fakir found sudden tears in his ice-clear eyes.

"And now I can take back my Lady's heart!" cried the Sculptor happily. "How I have longed for this day!"

"Wait, my friend," said the Fakir. "Something is amiss. Though we are victorious and I see your armor is still in place, even so you are still in bondage."

"Bondage? To whom?"

"That I cannot discern." The Fakir turned to the Girl. "But you hold his heart, perhaps it will be clearer to you."

"Indeed it is." She cast a winning smile at the Sculptor and held his gaze in her soft eyes. "Do you still not see? You have won her already."

"I know I have won her. Now come with me, we will take back her heart and build her anew."

She laid a precise finger on his lips and smiled again, a secret, delectable smile.

"You do not hear what you are saying, my heart. You have fallen under the power of your own gift. You saved my life and won my heart. Now it is my turn." And in a flash she snatched the white flute he carried and smashed it on the ground.

The Sculptor gasped as if drenched in ice water.

"You—" he pointed sharply at the shattered flute. Then his eyes opened, and he saw her. "You. It's you."

A boyish grin broke out on his face.

"It's you!" He gazed at her in curious wonder. "It's been you all along. There never was any life in that statue, was there?"

"None but a dim reflection of your own."

"But you! You are now flesh of my flesh—"

"—and bone of my bone." And her smile was

radiant, and her dark lovely hair swept about him as he lifted her and spun her around, and when she touched the ground her bright eyes caught his, and time ended and life began, and in that gaze was hope and longing and joy and passion and depth and laughter and best of all—

They kissed, and the Song surged through them, and they sang, together they sang, and their voices danced and their hearts soared, and they sang of beauty and joy and life, and lives poured into hearts entwined, and they sang of the Dreamer and the joy in his Dream and the exquisite beauty of all that he sang.

Soon they found that the whole camp was singing with them, and a great dance broke out, a leaping, whirling, joyous chaos of skipping children and swirling skirts and laughter and sunshine and rich thrilling song, until finally all sat back to rest, laughing and panting and chattering in tired excited stars of bodies stretched out on the young green grass. Two tiny children ran to the Lady and handed her a shield. It was made of shards of thin white marble held together with fine silver. It was a beautiful shield, thin as shell and sharp as shell and fine and strong and fierce and bright.

The Sculptor and his Singing Lady turned to the Fakir.

"The Dreamer calls us. We must go into the world to teach others the Song. Will you come with us?"

"No," he replied, and grinned as a beautiful little girl climbed into his lap. "My place is here, but wherever you go, remember that we always sing together."

He caught their eye, and they caught his, and all three smiled, for it was good.

"Now," declared the Lady, and her voice was dazzling, powerful, true, and the children looked on her and were awed.

A hush fell in the shimmering Song. The Sculptor felt his heart rejoice.

Wrapped up in wind, on new-born grass, the Singing Lady slowly stretched. She yawned precisely, smiled brightly, then winked at him and took his hand. They walked away as flesh and bone on spreading garden paths. The solemn children watched in gladness, some old and some young, some singing, some still. Each in his way gave fond farewells, with shout or song or smile or wave, and he, and Dreamer, and his Lady walked in fullness, life of life. Through her mouth the Song rang out and lives escaped the bonds of fear, and day by day he carved the shields of those the Dreamer saved through her. They taught the Song to all they met, and spread the dreamy streams of life, and night after day, and day after night, they followed the wind and ran to the light.

And as beauty spread the Sculptor walked with his bright Lady in the Dream. They spoke for hours, as heart to heart, and through the hours she listened with her lovely ears and laughed with her resplendent voice, and through the hours he listened close, and loved her song, and loved her heart. Then for a time they sang again, the music as ever strong and sweet, and finally the hour came, and she lay down in his arms, and smiled at him, and they dreamt.

THE END

Thanks for reading!

Reviews are one of the best ways to help get the word out to other readers, and they go a long way toward supporting the author. If you enjoyed *The Stone and the Song*, I'd love it if you'd take a minute or two to leave an online review and help others find it too. Thanks!

Ready for more?

Sign up for my email list at byfaroe.com/updates for news, production updates, and friendly notes. Or just drop me a line at byfaroe@gmail.com. I'd love to hear from you!

Keep reading for a sneak peek of *The Dream World Collective.*

Cheers!

Ben

Excerpt from **The Dream World Collective, a** *novel of friendship, romance, and geekery by Ben Y. Faroe*

7. Brilliant

Zen was on the roof, deep in his colorful hammock, with a travel mug of limeade in a hanging drink holder he'd rigged up, writing on a lap desk under a dramatic cloudy sky. He'd already done some serious writing that morning: an article interpreting the latest fad vampire novels as a sort of capitalist manifesto; a book review of a recent literary novel, *The Pendulum's Dilemma*; a third revision of his short story about a man who forgets how to read; and a few recipes for a cookbook he was starting to assemble. His three query letters for the day sat on the rooftop under a brick, ready to be mailed.

Now he climbed out, ruffled his pale blond hair in an absentminded way, and started pacing the roof, mumbling to himself, trying to figure out a concept that had been yanking at his innards for weeks now. He clattered down the fire escape and wandered out to go see Summer and Sushi.

A few burly guys in black t-shirts were moving books and boxes and cushions out of the building, leaving them in a big pile on the sidewalk. Zen waved vaguely as he drifted by. "What's going on?"

"Guys in 3A got evicted."

"Oh, interesting, interesting. Say hi to them for me."

Three blocks down the street, he rang the doorbell for Sushi and Summer's apartment. Sushi slammed the door open. "What?"

"Hey, you have any of that good pondering tea left? Put some on. There's ponderings afoot."

"Not now, Zen." She was already back at her easel, painting furiously.

"Cool, cool." He trundled into the kitchen, preoccupied with his thinking, and started making the tea. From the next room Sushi yelled at him.

"Go home!"

"Sure. Here's the thing. Why do we have jobs? Anyone, I mean? We complain about them so much. What do they even do?"

"Damned if I know. I say we just torch the place and go home."

"You ask anyone why they work if they hate their job so much, and they'll say they need the money, right?"

Sushi kept painting like she was hoping Zen would disappear if she ignored him. Zen continued.

"But all you get for the money is stuff. What if you could get the stuff without the money?"

"That's burglary. Hard jail time."

"No, if you just had fun making whatever you like making, and you traded it with people who wanted it."

"That's a medieval peasant system of barter. Plague. And overlords."

"What about living together with the other people and working together to make the stuff, everybody does the part they want?"

"Hippie commune. Funny-smelling deadbeats. And possibly plague again."

"Ooh, and sitars! I love sitars!" Zen strummed a huge air-sitar. "Brauunnmm." He flopped onto the ground, cross-legged, and took a thoughtful sip of his tea. "What if we made it deadbeat-free?"

"Pfff. With hippies? Good luck."

"Not with hippies. With us. We figure out crazy brilliant ways to have fun and make stuff we need, or money, or whatever. We could pull it off. Look, what are we all busting our butts at work for? Retirement? Why not just have the fun now?"

"Hmph." Zen could tell Sushi was growing interested despite herself. "What kind of fun?"

"All the stuff nobody does because they have to be back at work by Monday, or they're too tired from all the meetings and paperworks, or too nervous because they'd get fired."

"Or because their unprintable bosses are soul-sucking bastards who can't recognize real talent with two hands and a flashlight, especially when those hands are busy ogling—" She whacked paint at the canvas. "—blond—" Whack! "—wench—" Whack! "—interns!"

Zen was slightly taken aback.

"Yeah. Or that."

"Ok." Sushi stepped back, suddenly calmer. "Let's do it."

"What?"

"Do it. Make a commune. That's the thing, right? Everybody's always talking about how awesome it would be to do something awesome. Do it. I'm in. Let's go."

"Huh." Zen took a long sip of tea, pondering this. "We'd have to get the others in on it."

"Summer's in. She's always trying to do this kind of thing."

"Dude! We should get Otto, too. He could be our official technomage!"

"What about Alex?" asked Sushi.

"Harder. He's all...responsible. We'd have to find something that would really shake up—Wait a minute."

"What?"

Zen grinned and finished his tea in a great gulp.

"3A is us. Brilliant!" He turned to Sushi. "By the way, would you mind helping me move some things? I think it's starting to rain."

8. Advancement

Alex leaned against the wall, despite his better judgment. Steve walked into the back room.

"Professional bearing, Alex," Steve reminded him.

"Sorry." Alex straightened up and tried to look...busier.

"Have to set a good example for the underlings," laughed Steve in a corporate attempt at camaraderie.

Summer exploded into the back room, a tangle of backpack and visor and blushing apologies. Steve eloquently raised his eyebrows.

"I'll—" Summer hesitated, stowed her backpack under the coat hooks. "Go wipe the tables? Sorry to interrupt."

She brushed past them to go out behind the counter. Steve spoke up.

"Time card?"

"Oh, right. Sorry." Summer turned back to punch in, avoiding his eye. She flashed a pleading glance at Alex as she went back out. He returned it, sympathetic but pained. *What can I do?*

"She may have to go," observed Steve once Summer was out of earshot.

"Nah, she's all right most of the time."

"Seriously? I mean, did you see her there?"

Steve laughed, and the disrespect in his tone annoyed Alex.

"What? Late? That happens to all of us sometimes. No big deal."

"Not you. See, what I like about you is that you really understand what it takes to run a successful business." Steve's attempt at flattery was jarring, too transparent.

"I guess. But Summer's a good worker. She cares about people."

"Right."

"I'm serious. She's made friends with practically every customer who comes in during her shifts. She generates incredible brand loyalty."

Putting it in those terms made Alex feel a little dirty, as if the real point of good relationships was to generate business and not the other way around. But he had to use whatever was most likely to get through to Steve. One glance at his boss's sympathetic grimace showed him it hadn't worked, though.

"Look, I know she's your friend, Alex, but she's got to go."

"No, it's cool, man. I'll work with her. You know, give her a warning, make sure she straightens up. I've handled this sort of thing before."

"We've tried that already. She's just not working out."

"Steve, I can—"

"Sorry, Alex. If you're going to advance here, you need to show me you can put the store first. I'm telling you, as your boss. You need to fire Summer."

"Really? Just like that?"

"She had her chance."

Alex felt himself getting angry.

"Don't give me that, Steve. You can test me all you want, but don't bring a perfectly good worker's job into this."

Steve sighed.

"I've already made my assessment of her. She is going to lose her job, Alex. The only real question here is how much you care about yours."

"I see."

"It's not so bad after you get used to it. Firing people is just one of the necessities of the job. You'll understand once you've been in higher management for a while."

"How did you get into this line of work, Steve? Is it what you planned for in college?"

Steve laughed.

"No, I studied to be an architect, if you can believe it. Guess I was just in the right place at the right time. Corporate kept moving me up in the ranks, salary, benefits, the whole thing, and I certainly wasn't going to turn down a living like that. Pretty much the same as you, really."

"Wrong," said Alex. Steve glanced up, uncomprehending.

"What?"

"You're wrong. I'm giving my two weeks' notice."

"Over Summer? Alex, she's already gone."

Alex shrugged. Steve smiled his broad, ingratiating smile.

"Ok, you know what? Don't even worry about her. I'll take care of that myself."

"No, Steve. Sorry. I'm...going to head out. Mandy's got this shift under control."

Alex hung up his apron and found Summer wiping tables furiously.

"They're going to fire you," he said. "Just thought you should know."

Summer looked up sharply.

"What?"

"Sorry." He held her eye for a long moment, then smiled sadly. "It's ok. You don't deserve them."

Alex walked out into a light drizzle, and laughed.

When he arrived at home he found a buzz of activity, with Zen and Sushi and several neighbors carting books and electronics off the sidewalk, and covering a huge tumbled pile with tarps, garbage bags, and Zen's hammocks. Zen and Sushi were each hauling one end of a big trunk.

He grabbed Zen by the shoulder.

"What's going on?"

Zen laughed a trifle nervously.

"We got evicted. Destruction of property, apparently. I'm not sure what he's talking about."

Sushi broke in.

"Maybe your hammocks bolted all over the

walls? And the fire pit in the living room?"

"That was solid brick!" Zen protested. "And Alex made it all...smart. It didn't even get hot on the outsides."

"Yeah," Sushi shot back, "And I bet it did wonders for the hardwood floors."

Alex just stared at the pile of all their earthly belongings, then laughed darkly and spread his arms wide.

"It's a brand new day, gentlemen," he announced in an odd voice.

"And ladies," Sushi corrected him.

"And ladies," agreed Alex with a curious, almost sinister smile. "Tickled Pig, anyone? Drinks are on me."

And he stalked off into the rain.

Ready for even more?

Start from the beginning at bit.ly/startdwc. Then keep reading with more free sections of *The Dream World Collective* posted at bit.ly/latestdwc, and don't forget to sign up for updates and friendly notes at byfaroe.com/updates!

About the Author

Ben Y. Faroe lives in Baltimore, MD. He lives and writes as an apprentice of Jesus in community with his best friends. They feast together, drink good whiskey, push each other to do great creative work, and squeeze in board games when they can. That his wife and daughter are lovely beyond compare goes without saying.

This book is typeset in Gentium Basic and Gentium Book Basic.